USBORNE FIRST READING
Level One

USBORNE FIRST READING

The **Fox** and the **Crow**

Retold by Mairi Mackinnon
Illustrated by Rocío Martínez

USBORNE FIRST READING

The **Three Wishes**

Retold by Lesley Sims
Illustrated by Elisa Squillace

USBORNE FIRST READING

The **Lion** and the **Mouse**

Retold by Mairi Mackinnon
Illustrated by Frank Endersby

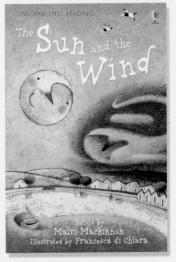

USBORNE FIRST READING

The **Sun** and the **Wind**

Retold by Mairi Mackinnon
Illustrated by Francesca di Chiara

Old MacDonald had a farm

Illustrated by Ben Mantle

Reading consultant: Alison Kelly
Roehampton University

Old MacDonald
had a farm, E-I-E-I-O.

3

And on his farm he had
some cows, E-I-E-I-O.

With a moo-moo here,

and a moo-moo there...

Here a moo,

there a
moo,

everywhere a moo-moo.

Old MacDonald had a farm, E-I-E-I-O.

And on his farm he had
some sheep, E-I-E-I-O.

With a baa-baa here,

and a baa-baa there...

11

Here a baa,

there a baa,

everywhere
a baa-baa.

Old MacDonald had
a farm, E-I-E-I-O.

And on his farm he had
some pigs, E-I-E-I-O.

With an oink-oink here,

and an oink-oink there...

17

Here an oink,

there an oink,

18

everywhere an oink-oink.

Old MacDonald had a farm, E-I-E-I-O.

And on his farm
he had some hens,

E-I-E-I-O.

With a cluck-cluck here,

and a cluck-cluck there...

Here a cluck,

there
a cluck,

everywhere a
cluck-cluck.

PUZZLES

Puzzle 1

Can you spot the differences between these two pictures?

There are six to find.

What happened next?

Puzzle 2

A

or

B

Puzzle 3

A

or

B

Puzzle 4
Find these things in the picture:

bucket	house	tails
sun	butterfly	boot

Answers to puzzles

Puzzle 1

Puzzle 2

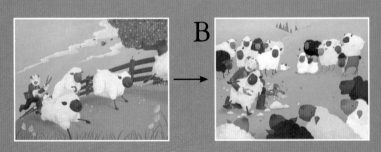

B

Puzzle 3

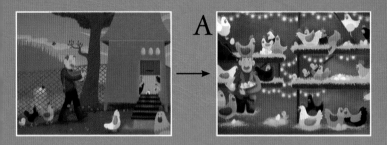

A

Puzzle 4

sun

house

butterfly

tails

boot

bucket

Designed by Caroline Spatz
Edited by Felicity Parker
Series designer: Russell Punter
Series editor: Lesley Sims

First published in 2009 by Usborne Publishing Ltd., Usborne House, 83-85 Saffron Hill, London EC1N 8RT, England. www.usborne.com
Copyright © 2009 Usborne Publishing Ltd.

USBORNE FIRST READING
Level Two

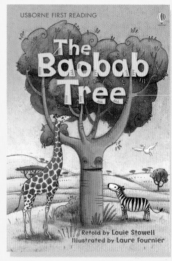

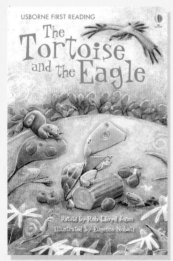